# LUCY MAUD
## *and the*
# CAVENDISH CAT

LYNN MANUEL

ILLUSTRATED BY JANET WILSON

TUNDRA BOOKS

This story has been adapted from *The Selected Journals of L. M. Montgomery*, Volumes I and II, edited by Mary Rubio and Elizabeth Waterston, Oxford University Press (1985 & 1987).

Permission to adapt material from *The Selected Journals of L. M. Montgomery*, author of *Anne of Green Gables*, has been granted by Mary Rubio, Elizabeth Waterston, and the University of Guelph, courtesy of the L. M. Montgomery Collection Archives and Special Collections, University of Guelph Library, with the approval of the Heirs of L. M. Montgomery.

Published in Canada by Tundra Books, *McClelland & Stewart Young Readers*, 481 University Avenue, Toronto, Ontario M5G 2E9

Published in the United States by Tundra Books of Northern New York, P.O. Box 1030, Plattsburgh, New York 12901

Library of Congress Catalog Number: 97-60483

Canadian Cataloguing in Publication Data

Manuel, Lynn
    Lucy Maud and the Cavendish cat

ISBN 0-88776-397-9

1. Montgomery, L. M. (Lucy Maud), 1874-1942 – Juvenile fiction.
I. Wilson, Janet, 1952-   . II. Title.

PS8576.A57L82 1997     jC813 '.54     C97-930629-9
PZ7.M36Lu 1997

We acknowledge the support of the Canada Council for the Arts for our publishing program.

Design: Sari Ginsberg

Printed and bound in Canada

1 2 3 4 5 6          02 01 00 99 98 97

*T*o Jenny, May your life be filled
with love and laughter
L.M.

To Sarah, Elizabeth, and
Marjorie, my Musselburgh cats,
with great affection
J.W.

*The illustrator expresses heartfelt
thanks for the generous help and
co-operation of Dawn and Micio,
her models, and Mary Rubio,
her Lucy Maud expert.*

$O$nce he had been Daffy, the Cavendish cat, but now he was just poor little Daffy, the castoff, sitting in the mousy loft of a barn that was not his own, listening to the trees at Park Corner swish in the wind, the way Maud's long skirts used to swish when she came down the stairs.

And the spot ached where he had pinned her to his heart.

*I*t was a spring day long ago when he first heard Maud's voice drifting through the patchwork quilt of shadows inside Alec Macneill's barn.

"The only real cat is a gray cat," she said as she picked him out, the grayest of the grays, from the batch of new kittens, peering at him through her spectacles while he peered back through his squinty kitten eyes.

Then, quick as a wink, he was inside a covered basket, howling up a storm as she carried him home on her arm.

*D*affy tried and tried to scrape up an acquaintance with the grandmother who was old and deaf and hated cats, but she was as stiff and prickly as a porcupine. There was one time in particular when she had looked up from her sweeping, and with a hand cupped over her ear, had creaked, "Eh?"

"I do so love a cat to purr," Maud said, with a bit of a shout, "It's the most comfortable sound in nature."

"Hmph!" Her bristly broom was coming closer and closer. "This one can't even do that, except when he's hungry." Then all of a sudden the grandmother swooshed him right out the door, along with the bread crumbs. "Cats belong outside at night!"

But Daffy found a way to outwit her by climbing onto the kitchen roof, then slipping through the open window of the north room, and scurrying down the hall to curl up on the white coverlet atop Maud's bed.

*S*ometimes Maud would read to him from the story she was scribbling, the story of an elderly couple who apply to an orphan asylum for a boy, and get a girl instead. And her voice would murmur late into the night until the oil almost burned out of the lamp.

*N*ow and again, Daffy went along on her photographing expeditions, prowling for mice in the hayfields while she prowled about with her camera. And if she disappeared for one of her lonely walks, he would always wait for her to come back, springing down from the fence and scampering about her feet as she turned into the old lane.

"I don't think I shall feel perfectly at home in heaven if there are no adorable kittens frisking about!" she said, laughing whenever she saw him.

*I*n the evenings, her pen would scratch like a branch against the windowpanes, or her fingers would peg away with a click-click-click of the keys on the old typewriter that didn't make the capitals plain and wouldn't print "w" at all. And all the while Daffy would doze at her feet, while the grandmother sewed or read at the other side of the kitchen table.

Maud's fingers would tremble whenever she tied up her bundle of scribbling for the publishers. "Something may come of my pen yet, Daffins," she said.

But the bundle came back again and again, until finally she tucked it away in an old hatbox in the north room. "Not to worry, I still have a lovely gray cat."

*T*he windows had grown thick with frost and snow. No birds trilled. No crickets nor frogs sang. The only sound was the shrieking of the icy wind in the eaves. The house was so cold, it was not fit to live in. The grandmother would allow a fire only in the kitchen.

When the huge drifts made prisoners of them, Daffy saw the sadness in Maud's eyes. He watched as she began to fold in upon herself, corner-to-corner and end-to-end, as the lonely winter dragged on. He knew she missed having the run of the red-clover fields and the woods with its ferny nooks and hollows. She missed the sweet-smelling grass as much as he did.

*D*affy wanted to do something to make her eyes shine again, and one day his chance came when Maud was rummaging in the north room for a blanket. "It's blowing a hurricane and spitting snow out there!" she said. That's when he curled up in the old hatbox and refused to budge until she finally scooped him out. "Run along, Daff-o-dil! You know you much prefer a cushion or a rocking chair to a hatbox full of scribbling!"

She glanced down then at her story and began to shuffle the pages, pausing to read here and there. "Maybe I'll try sending it out again." Daffy gave a little leap of pleasure at her words.

This time the bundle did not come back. Instead, a letter arrived from the L.C. Page Company of Boston. Oh, how Maud's eyes sparkled behind her spectacles when she read that letter again and again to him!

"*Anne of Green Gables* will be a real live book, Daff. My very own! What do you think of that?" It didn't matter that he had no words for her. He simply chased his tail around and around and around.

*B*ut everything changed when the grandmother became ill.

"Where's Daffy?"

The grandmother-who-hated-cats was asking for him, stroking his gray fur and murmuring softly, "Poor little Daffy! Poor little Daffy!" Then she closed her eyes for the last time.

Furniture was given away. Pictures were packed. Maud carried him from their home the way he had arrived, in a covered basket on her arm, whispering, "I don't think I shall be able to scribble if I'm not in Cavendish!"

And so they came to this place called Park Corner to stay with relatives who were strangers to him – and one was a little boy who lugged cats about upside-down!

The day arrived when Maud came down the stairs in a mist of white with an orange-blossom wreath in her hair. It was the day she said good-bye, and left with the man who was now her husband. It was the day she left the Cavendish cat behind.

*S*itting in the mousy loft of a barn that was not his own, Daffy looked up into the night sky and remembered his very own chipped saucer with its very own ancient tea stains, a silvery-white moon of milk on the kitchen floor. He remembered the red door, the yellow light in the window, and the old grandmother sitting in her worn-out chair by the table, a gray shawl wrapped around her shoulders. He remembered Maud's pen scratching.

Then one day, the strangers came looking for him. They shut him in a box and they wouldn't let him out when he shrieked.

*T*here was food, but he didn't eat. The box jiggled and rocked, thumped and hopped. There was a clanging and a hissing and a whistling. Daffy peered through the slit at the top, but he couldn't see where they were taking him. He shrieked until he could shriek no more, and finally, he curled up with his paws beneath him and folded in upon himself, corner-to-corner and end-to-end.

*T*ime went by like the slow meandering of a cow across Sam Wyand's field as Daffy's thoughts turned to the old well where the ferns grew all around and the darkness waited. He was certain that's where he must be, down deep inside, without anyone to lower a bucket. Maud had disappeared in a white-silk mist, leaving him all alone.

An eternity passed before he looked up and saw the eyes behind the spectacles, and quick as a wink, he was in Maud's arms.

"My lovely, gray cat!" And Maud was laughing and crying all at the same time.

*D*affy lapped up milk from his very own chipped saucer with its very own ancient tea stains in his new home in Ontario. And when he heard the scratching of a pen, the Cavendish cat leaped into Maud's lap and began to purr.

# AUTHOR'S NOTE

LUCY MAUD MONTGOMERY was born in Clifton (now New London), Prince Edward Island on November 30, 1874. After her mother died, Maud lived in Cavendish with her grandparents, Alexander and Lucy Macneill. Daffy was with her through the most important times of her life – her sudden rise to fame as the author of *Anne of Green Gables*, her marriage, and the birth of her children. As the years passed, he became her "last living link" to her old life, and whenever she saw him curled up on his cushion, she would remember her beloved Cavendish home. When he died at the ripe old age of fourteen, Maud mourned deeply for him. He was buried behind the asparagus patch on the family lawn in Leaskdale, Ontario.

*Lucy Maud and the Cavendish Cat* is a true story, compiled from the many references to Daffy that appear in the *Selected Journals of L. M. Montgomery, Volumes I and II*. In most instances, the words that Maud speaks are her own thoughts as expressed in the journals.

A tuft of fur from Daffy, the Cavendish cat, can be seen in one of Maud's scrapbooks now on display at the L. M. Montgomery Museum in New London, Prince Edward Island.